To my brother Gérard!—F. P.

To my Titi—A. P

FRED PARONUZZI

Fred Paronuzzi was born in 1967 in Savoy, France. He traveled around the world for ten years and taught French in Canada, Scotland, and Slovakia, before returning to his birthplace. Fred writes for both adults and children—including novels, picture books, and more recently comic books. His books have been translated into Russian, German, Portuguese, and now English. *Babak the Beetle* is his first collaboration with Andrée Prigent.

ANDRÉE PRIGENT

Andrée Prigent was born in 1963 in Brest, France. She studied at the Regional School of Fine Arts of Rennes, where she focused on graphic art. Andrée has since illustrated for publishers, newspapers, and magazines. She has also created designs for fabrics, games, dishes, and clocks. She lives in Rennes, France.

English translation copyright © 2016 by NorthSouth Books, Inc., New York 10016.
First published in France under the title GÉRARD LE BOUSIER.
GÉRARD LE BOUSIER (text and illustrations) copyright © 2014 by Kaleidoscope, France.
English translation by Elie Brangbour.

All rights reserved. No part of this book may be reproduced or utilized in any form
or by any means, electronic or mechanical, including photo-copying, recording,
or any information storage and retrieval system, without permission in writing from
the publisher.

First published in the United States and Canada in 2016 by NorthSouth Books, Inc.,
an imprint of Nord-Süd Verlag AG, CH-8005 Zürich, Switzerland.
Distributed in the United States by NorthSouth Books, Inc., New York 10016.
Library of Congress Cataloging-in-Publication Data is available.
ISBN: 978-0-7358-4251-9
Printed in Latvia by Livonia Print, Riga, November 2015.
1 3 5 7 9 · 10 8 6 4 2
www.northsouth.com

MIX
Paper from responsible sources
FSC® C002795

BABAK
THE BEETLE

By **Fred Paronuzzi**

Illustrated by
Andrée Prigent

North South

One morning, Babak was on his way home, rolling
a magnificent dung ball, when suddenly . . .

BUMP!

"Uh-oh! That looks like an egg. Did somebody lose it?
If I leave it here, someone will eat it. I must find
its owner. Obviously, an egg needs to be sat on!"

And so the brave dung beetle left his dung ball behind
and set off immediately.

He rolled the egg for a long time under the
hot sun without meeting anyone until . . .
"Ahem?"
"Is someone calling me? Oh, it's you, little
dung beetle. . . Might I be of assistance?"

"I hope so, Mrs. Ostrich.
You see, I am looking for this egg's parents."

"It's a strange one, isn't it? It's all dented!
You could fit ten of those in just one of mine!
It's not from around here, that's for sure.
Here's my advice: go to the woods where there
are plenty of birds. You'll find someone there
to help you."

"Excellent idea! Thank you, Mrs. Ostrich!"

Babak started off again and walked for a long time through the savanna before entering the woods.
"It will be really surprising if I don't find my egg's mom or dad among all these birds. But I need to get their attention."

He wriggled around like a puppet, doing it so well that a cuckoo spotted him and flew down to meet him.

"Do you need anything, little dung beetle?"

"Yes, I do, Mr. Cuckoo. Tell me, do you know the parents of this egg?"

"Well, son, you've asked a specialist! I'm sure you know that cuckoos don't sit on their own eggs but put them in other birds' nests, . . . so you can imagine I am familiar with many kinds of eggs!

"Alas, I can't help you, for without a doubt, this is not a bird's egg. . . You might have more luck over by the swamp."

"Thank you very much, Mr. Cuckoo!"

And off went Babak, tirelessly rolling the decidedly mysterious egg. Soon the ground became as soggy as a sponge, and a deafening concert could be heard:

Ribbit! Ribbit! Ribbit!

"Um, excuse me, Mrs. Frog, but I have an egg here, and I'm searching for its family. . ."

"An egg? Just one? Ha, ha, ha! My friend, you should know that I lay thousands of eggs . . . in big, transparent piles! You can even see my children inside them. Look!"

Babak was very impressed . . . but also a little sickened because they looked like jelly eyes.

"Yours is probably a snake's egg. You'll find the snakes at the foot of the hill. . . But beware that they don't swallow you whole!"

"Thanks for the advice, Mrs. Frog!" Babak was getting tired. "At this rate, I'm going to go around the world!" But, gathering all his courage, he zigzagged between the stones and reached the large rocks where a bunch of tangled-up snakes were lounging in the sun.

"Um . . . please excuse me, ladies and gentlemen, but I found an egg. Would it be one of yours by any chance?"

"Let me see, little dung beetle. Hmmm. No, I'm sorry; our eggs are smooth and elongated. But I do know where this one comes from. I swallowed one once, and I never did digest it. It was at the edge of those large fields over there."

"Oh, thank you for this helpful information, Mrs. Snake!"

Babak set off again reinvigorated, crossing a bridge and sliding into a thicket near some freshly cut grass.

There he saw heaps of eggs like his. The grass was covered with them, but . . . but . . .

how awful!

The parents of the eggs, armed with long sticks, were hitting the eggs and sending them off, flying through the air! Again and again, until the eggs fell into holes!

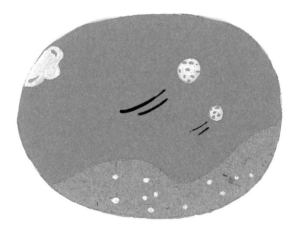

What a horrible sight!

Babak was devastated. "They're crazy; that is no way
to behave! What brutes! I will NOT give my egg to such
savages. . . . I will take it home with me, and if I must,
I will learn how to hatch an egg!"

And Babak took off as fast as he could . . . very happy
to keep this egg that he really, really, really no longer
wanted to give away!